The Roly-Poly Rice Ball

A Japanese fairy tale

Retold by Rosie Dickins
Illustrated by Ben Mantle

Reading consultant: Alison Kelly
Roehampton University

This story is about
a poor woodcutter
named Miki,

a roly-poly rice ball

and some magic mice.

Miki had no money.
He had hardly any food.

He rolled the rice into a roly-poly ball.

He wrapped it up.

And he set off for work.

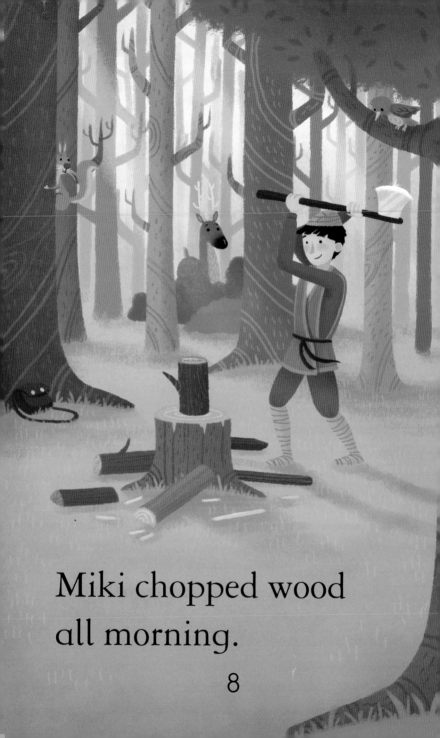

Miki chopped wood
all morning.

By lunchtime he was very, very hungry.

So he took out
the rice ball.

Oh no!

It rolled out of his
hands and into a hole.

Miki reached after it...

He tumbled in too.

He landed in a cave
lit by tiny lanterns.

13

There were lots of mice.
They began to sing.

A roly-poly rice ball,
A roly-poly treat,

Roll away, roll away,
Here for us to eat.

Miki smiled.

The mice had made his rice into tiny cakes.

"Come and join our
feast," they squeaked.

17

So Miki did. He ate and sang and danced...

A roly-poly rice ball,
A roly-poly treat...

At last, it was time
to go home.

The mice thanked Miki
for his rice.

"Now we have a gift for
you," they squeaked.

It was a little
golden spoon.

21

Miki waved the spoon.
Gold coins rained down.

He waved it again. A
bowl of rice appeared.

It must
be magic!

With the magic spoon,
Miki was never poor or
hungry again.

Puzzles

Puzzle 1

Look at the pictures and put them in order:

A

B

C

D

Puzzle 2

Find the words to finish
the song.

poly   roll   eat   rice

A roly-poly ___ ball,
A roly-___ treat,
Roll away, ___ away,
Here for us to ___.

Puzzle 3

Can you spot the differences
between these two pictures?

There are six to find.

Answers to puzzles

Puzzle 1 - C A D B

 C

 A

 D

 B

Puzzle 2

A roly-poly rice ball,
A roly-poly treat,
Roll away, roll away,
Here for us to eat.

Puzzle 3

About the story

The Roly-Poly Rice Ball is a traditional tale from Japan. In Japan, rice balls are a popular snack.

Designed by Caroline Spatz
Series designer: Russell Punter
Series editor: Lesley Sims

First published in 2011 by Usborne Publishing Ltd., Usborne House, 83-85 Saffron Hill, London EC1N 8RT, England. www.usborne.com
Copyright © 2011 Usborne Publishing Ltd.

USBORNE FIRST READING
Level Three

Noah's Ark
Retold by Katie Daynes
Illustrated by John Joven

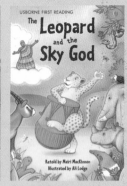

The Leopard and the Sky God
Retold by Mairi MacKinnon
Illustrated by Ali Lodge

frogs
Sarah Courtauld
Illustrated by Jacqueline East

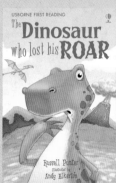

The Dinosaur who lost his ROAR
Russell Punter
Illustrated by Andy Elkerton

The Peach Boy
Retold by Alex Frith
Illustrated by Kelly Murphy

The Mouse's Wedding
Retold by Mairi MacKinnon
Illustrated by Frank Endersby

The Musicians of Bremen
Retold by Susanna Davidson
Illustrated by Mike Gordon

Bugs
Sarah Courtauld
Illustrated by Daniela Scarpa

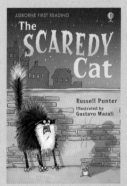

The SCAREDY Cat
Russell Punter
Illustrated by Gustavo Mazali